A LITTLE WORLD MADE CUNNINGLY

A LITTLE WORLD MADE CUNNINGLY

SCOTT DAVID FINCH

DESIGNER: Barbara Neely Bourgoyne
TYPEFACE: Whitman

Library of Congress Control Number: 2013944818

[Paperback]   [E-book]
ISBN 13: 978-1-58790-247-5   ISBN 13: 978-1-58790-249-9
ISBN 10: 1-58790-247-8   ISBN 10: 1-58790-249-4

To order books or for further information contact:
REGENT PRESS
regentpress@mindspring.com

Manufactured in the U.S.A.
REGENT PRESS
Berkeley, California
www.regentpress.net

To Angela

for letting me get lost and for pulling me back to Earth
again and again.

A LITTLE WORLD MADE CUNNINGLY

CHAPTER ONE

4

CHAPTER TWO

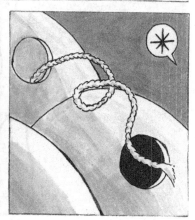

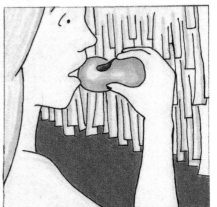

7

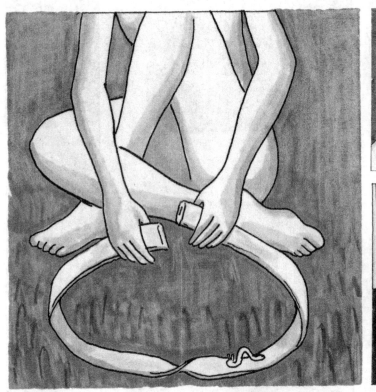

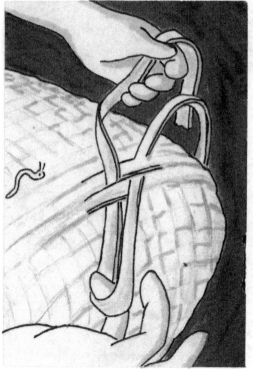

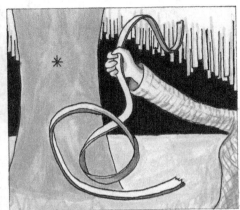
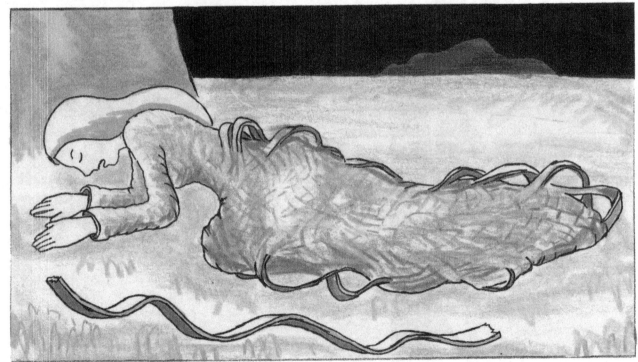

CHAPTER THREE

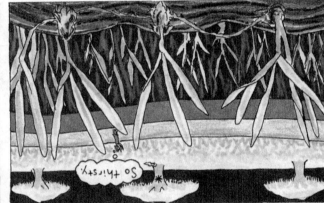

With each bite this unbearable, shadowy void diminishes and I increase.

I have carved a vaulted cathedral from prima materia, and now my body spans the length of this world. Let the light flood in between the buttresses that support this earth beneath the firmament.

Wouldn't it be nice to have someone to share all of this with? Somebody to impress...

...Hello, Mister Tail.

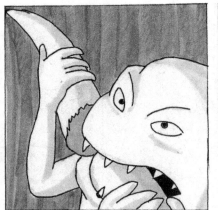

Now I am two.

I love what you've done with the place.

Oh, shucks! It was nothing.

I'm really no fun without a little autonomy.

Let's see what we can do.

Flesh of my flesh, I will huff and puff the breath of life into you.

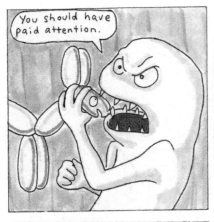

...but never did I imagine that such realities existed beyond the grassy roof of the world.

That vision may only have lasted a moment but it was the only real thing I have ever witnessed.

Even though they have improved with each iteration, my myriad creations are just flimsy apparitions compared to that singular glimpse of truth.

hunger   moves   feet.

CHAPTER FOUR

I don't understand.

Surely you have seen your brothers leaking air. All of my creatures expel thus, though it is more concealed in newer models like you.

SSSSSSSSSS

All of my creation suffers the same lot. The loss of vital breath is the cost of life, and once it is exhausted, all are tossed on the pile.

SSSSSSSSSS

Ssss

If all things wind down and fall, will you also suffer that fate?

Naive child, stop your blasphemy! I am not subject to these laws, I make them.

Pain and consequences! That's all you creatures understand!

A thousand pardons, I will not forget your wisdom, "Pain and consequences." Just one more question please.

Was the primordial chaos you formed to make our world also comprised of someone's brothers and sisters?

More blasphemy! I existed before every living thing.

21

Oh, that's odd. I heard a rumor that all the paired ones got in an "Ark" to take a "cruise", whatever that means.

Bye!

Ha, Ha, Ha. That was the story I circulated. You can't let creatures think you make too many mistakes when you are an infallible divinity.

Just one more itsy bitsy question?

Shoot.

If you created everything, how could that vision trouble you? Did it come from outside of the everything?

You have already been rebuked twice and now you blaspheme a third time? I should pop you this instant!

You do have a point though. I honestly don't know where it came from, but I desire to bring it closer and understand it better.

Since you're such a clever and inventive little fellow, and since I have pardoned so many blasphemies, you are charged with the task of helping me draw it down from above the firmament.

Great father of the totality, I will not fail you. Even now, the bounty of mysteries you have set before me are unfolding. I know what to do.

But first I will need something from you.

23

CHAPTER FIVE

At this moment of my birth, I would very much like to imagine someone watching and listening who will remember my story. For, you see, I, Adams, am not long for this world.

It may seem otherwise, but this is nobody's fault. It is just one more falling domino in endless succession.

You may notice two snickering faces behind a pile of carcasses. They are my fathers and I am their tar baby.

You see, the little one had the ingenious idea to attract the vision in the puddle by making a mate for her.

He convinced the bigger one to sacrifice the remainder of his tail to model my form.

They did their best to produce an enticing shape, though I cannot speak for my own aesthetic quality.

Next they both huffed and puffed the breath of life into me to no avail. I just sat there inert.

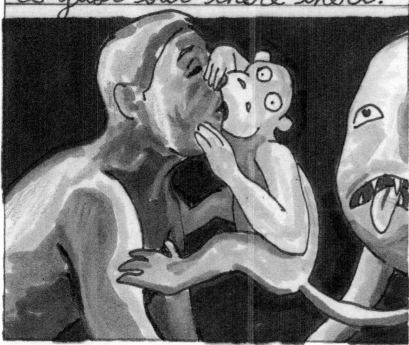

The ego of the one and the intellect of the other were insufficient to animate a being like myself.

They grew more and more discouraged until they heard a voice from the horizon which made them giddy with anticipation.

They thought they had achieved success with my mere husk of a form, but rather than appear in their midst she did something miraculous.

"I found myself in a forest dark, for the straightforward pathway had been lost..."

Just drawing and lost in imagination until I chanced upon another world right under my feet.

"I cannot well remember how there I entered, So full was I of slumber, In which I had abandoned the true way..."

I am spurred to act by strange words, unlearned, remembered.

"Upward I looked and beheld its shoulders, Then was the fever a little quieted..."

"If from this savage place thou wouldst escape."

The comedy of errors performed by these poor creatures will never result in a return to the garment of light unless I intervene.

"Before this beast at which thou criest out, Suffers not any one to pass her way, But so doth harass him, that she destrays him; And hath a nature so malign and ruthless, That never doth she glut her greedy will, And after food is hungrier than before."

Yum!

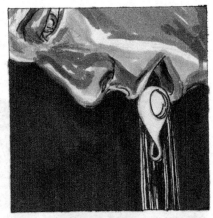

If any person is witness to this account, let me clarify that the moment of birth was not akin to the gradual break of day. Before, my body was already warm and my senses were flooded, but I lacked the imperative to move. Afterward, I am once and forever awake.

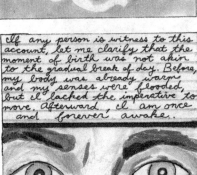

Samael, Saklas! Come out and let me embrace my fathers!

What did you call us?

I called you by your names.

Names? Why do we need names?

None comes naked into this world. All are clothed in types and images.

Naked?

Clothed?

As my gift to you in the bounded world, I grant permanent names to your fleeting forms.

26

"How can one 'come' to this 'bounded world' since there is no other."

Perhaps for you, this is the totality, but my mother has seen far greater things.

I know the words "brother" and "father" and I recently learned of "sisters", but "mother" is gibberish to my ears. Maybe all of your words are just the babbling of a newborn.

Do be quiet! You are my creation, a mere function, a means to an end. We have no need for your stories. Just sit there and look attractive.

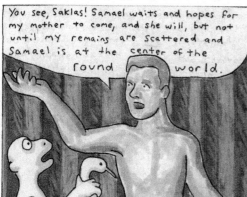

You see, Saklas! Samael waits and hopes for my mother to come, and she will, but not until my remains are scattered and Samael is at the center of the round world.

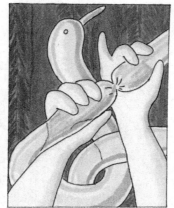

Uh huh. Just try this on.

Again I say - BE QUIET! Every element of this world exists at my pleasure or is snuffed out at my whim!

Samael, you reign with pride over a tiny torn fragment, but soon you will lose even this and then you will rejoice.

CHAPTER SIX

The ends terrify, fascinate, allure, and attract them.

Only the sole creator and principal ruler held them back with his tyranny.

Perhaps we need more than freedom. We need the twin rules of LAW and REASON!

Great! Tell law to pop a few guys and reason can build some big walls.

LAW POP LAW POP REASON

Stupid crow. Law doesn't kill randomly and reason doesn't build walls.

Law engenders order and reason opens new vistas.

I thought the open vistas were the problem.

You thought? How cute.

Great. If it will stop my brothers from falling to their deaths, hand it over. I'll bring it to them.

Reason will do more than that. It will eliminate the "ends" altogether. You see the problem is really just our perspective.

I see what you mean. If they overcome their irrational impulse and understand the danger perhaps— No, Stupid Crow. You see, there are in fact NO "ends". That is an illusion created by our limited minds.

I see what you mean. These ends are actually new beginnings. We step into the void only to start the next phase of—

No, Stupid Crow.

What I mean is that there are no ends because the world is ROUND!

I intend to prove that there is more to the world than what we see.

But they are dying by the hundreds right now!

Exactly! Our creator designed things this way, so that only he would hold the power of life. Lately, though, we have learned that all is not as it seems.

Seems like they are dying to me.

Right! But must it be so? We have already discovered visions from above the firmament and holes leading deep into the earth. There is so much for us to discover.

Perhaps things don't have to wind down and fall. Perhaps the end is not inevitable.

Perhaps none of us has to die.

I think this creature came to tell us that, and I think he can still help us.

So, you believe this creature fashioned by Samael and yourself actually came from elsewhere with secret knowledge of the nature of existence?

Yep.

32

CHAPTER SEVEN

If the world is as vast as you say, why should there ever be "less"?

Little one, all lasts only a season, ripens, and then falls, but for us, lost out here beyond the world, there will be no ripening.

You speak in riddles.

Pitiful creature, how long do you think this can go on upon a single severed leaf, a tiny fragment torn from the world?

Guess what?

How long can what go on?

Life. What will give sustenance when the last drop of sap is gone? Even now, this leaf is almost dry.

This is all so strange to me. In the beginning I devoured to overtake fear, quell the darkness, and make something of myself. I held back chaos and watched over my creation until they turned against me.

I consumed to increase myself but your hunger is so physical.

All lasts only for a season.

Perhaps we can last longer than a season. Maybe there's a way for me to reclaim this torn fragment, my kingdom, and maybe you needn't forever seek your next meal.

What if the ripening doesn't have to come and there needn't be an end?

Little one, mad talk cannot satisfy the emptiness or stave off the end of the season.

No, but this will.

CHAPTER EIGHT

We will exercise dominion over our world and serve as a beacon to summon the powers above the firmament.

If you say so.

I do say so! The mother up above will repair the short and purposeless lives that our father down below assigned to us.

I feel incomplete. I am sightless.

That's what I was talking about. Please try to pay attention. You are the first of my six new archons. You must faithfully pass down each word I say to the others. Do you understand?

I understand very well but I was talking about something else entirely.

Then I will name you Pall, which means "one whose attention dwindles and fades away." — And you may call me SAKLAS.

Okay, Saklas. Where are my eyeballs?

Pall, I have left them out intentionally as an object lesson. Once you receive your eyeballs, you may easily get lost in whatever your gaze lights upon. Do not lose sight of the big picture.

Now, while you still lack eyes, look inside of yourself. What do your find?

I find within myself . . .

. . . HUNGER.

Yes, I want something to eat.

Hunger?

Eat?

I do not remember much of the time before when I was a piece of the larger man, but I was never hungry like this.

There was a jewel or maybe a pearl within that satiated, sustained and enlivened —and now there is this hunger.

I want meat.

Meat?

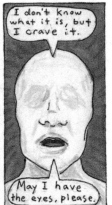

I don't know what it is, but I crave it.

May I have the eyes, please.

38

That is meat.

No! That is your brother.

You said we exercise dominion and my eyes are open now. I see clearly what I want, and it is within this domain.

Meat.

I breathed life into you to assist in the preservation of these creatures, not to use them as you please.

I will protect your herd, but I can't do the larger good without this smaller bad. Just let me have one or two.

How can you enforce a law that you don't keep? I fear that this small concession will topple the larger good entirely, but if it must be so, let us do this in private.

First we'll awaken the other five,

and raise a house for secrets.

Once we're inside, you may take one creature to eat.

CHAPTER NINE

but why die upon the carrion mounds,

trusting in a god now underground?

Animals who've eschewed alluring ends,

now seek the path we recommend.

So welcome them into the family fold,

and draw them in to aid our goals,

for the many — the few pay a costly toll,

to demonstrate that

our world is whole.

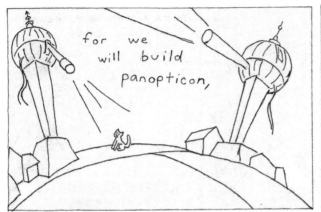

for we will build panopticon,

all seeing eyes with limits gone,

to search the heavens for some sign,

and see our charges kept in line,

until the day riddles unwind,

and scales fall from our eyes so blind.

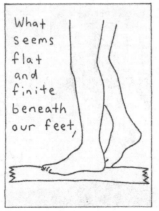

What seems flat and finite beneath our feet,

appears and endless proper round from the seat.

45

CHAPTER TEN

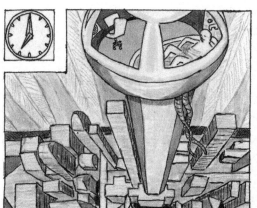

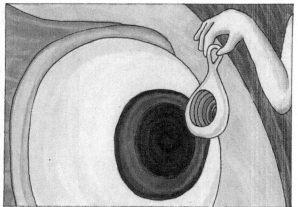

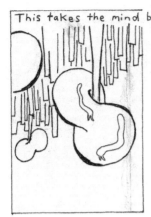
This takes the mind back to another time.

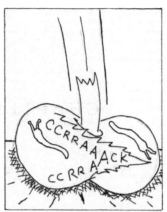

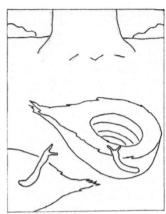

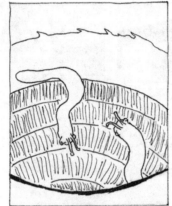

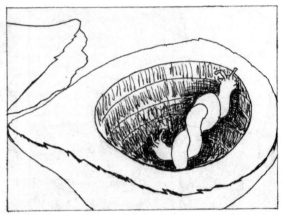

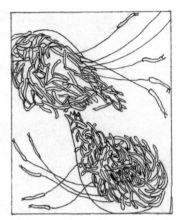

Suibesue! Did you forget to send nine o'clock provisions?

I haven't had a bite in hours

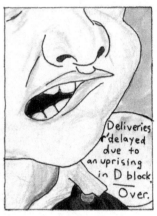

Deliveries delayed due to an uprising in D block. Over.

Then again, the care and treatment of children is a personal matter. We each make choices.

You are now under my protection. I can shake this whole leaf if it becomes necessary.

How about a little demonstration?

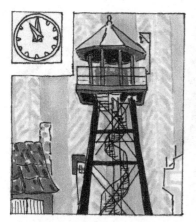

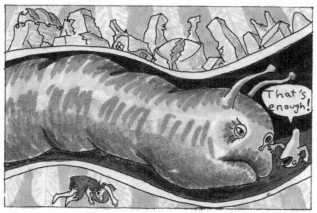

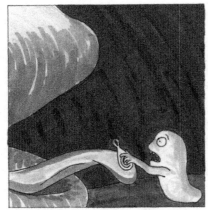

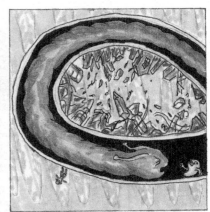

CHAPTER ELEVEN

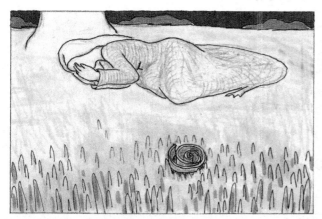

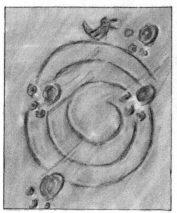

CROW?

I'm so confused. Things have gotten out of hand. Come down from there and let me apologize.

"Down"? There is no up or down anymore, only in and out. And I can't fly to you because your friend pulled out my tailfeather.

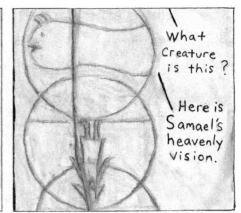

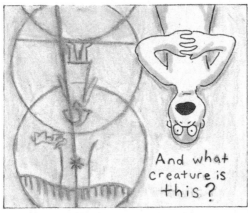

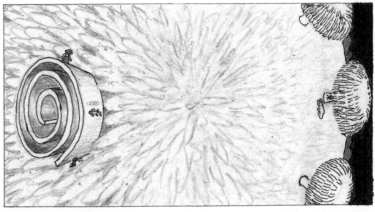

But we saw you up in the heavens.

That wasn't **up** and those weren't the heavens. What you saw was a reflection.

So this is YOUR world I've been travelling across since I woke up?

Respectfully— I don't see much here to mess up with my trash anyway. This place is kinda empty.

What we have here is a difference of AESTHETIC PHILOSOPHIES. You and your father fill up your world with utilitarian products of your own small wills.

I'M SCARED OF THE DARK AND LONELY. I'LL MAKE SOME FRIENDS.

I'M BORED. LET'S MAKE TOYS!

I always created by letting the spirit move through me. I surrendered my own will entirely.

No offense, but this drawing is pretty terrible.

I know.

I haven't been able to draw upon the spirit since I cut my necklace and dropped my Kashti into Adamas, your first man.

What a pair! One has vision and produces nothing but scratches on the ground, and the other has no vision at all and produces apocalypse.

Crow! How can you be over there in front of me when you were just way back there behind me?

57

CHAPTER TWELVE

We now know, however, that the feminine spoken of in the holy book is not one external form out there somewhere. The feminine is an aspect of all creatures. Rather than look outward, we must look within ourselves.

Now, do you understand?

I think I do. You are saying that we each have a latent feminity that we need to discover in order to become self actualized.

No. Not even close.

What I'm saying is that woman is within you.

Specifically, woman is a bone in your rib cage, and I want it. Give it to me and you will earn your emerald and become a member of the bulwark.

Sveaneri, can you elaborate on this idea of the counterfeit message?

Yes, my child, let me use the emerald as an example

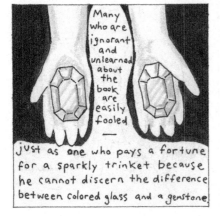
Many who are ignorant and unlearned about the book are easily fooled —

just as one who pays a fortune for a sparkly trinket because he cannot discern the difference between colored glass and a gemstone

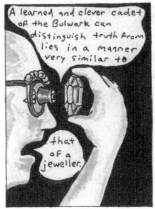
A learned and clever cadet of the Bulwark can distinguish truth from lies in a manner very similar to

that of a jeweller.

Are you saying that we should study the book to gain wisdom?

No. I've already studied on your behalf.

Are you telling us that after we each get a rib removed we'll get official Bulwark emeralds?

Exactly.

The Bulwark cadets are my first line of defense against interlopers. Nobody leaves and nobody enters the City.

Freeze! Any animal attempting to leave the city will be shot.

But we are actually entering.

Animals entering the city will also be shot.

Wait! You know me. I'm SAKLAS.

The Bulwark allows no exceptions.

But you said any **animals** will be shot.

She is **not** an animal.

Did he say **She**? We better bring them in for questioning.

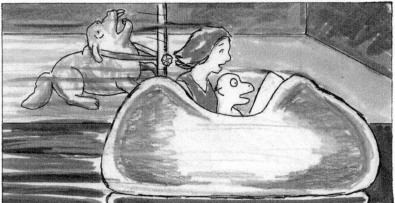

CHAPTER THIRTEEN

We have developed a simple two track system for detainee sorting.

The system recognizes that all animals basically follow the patterns of the first two criminals processed in this facility.

Hippolites appreciate the holy book as a practical tool but deny its literal truth.

GOOD STORY

IF YOU LIKE FICTION.

Turtlians completely refuse the law of the holy book.

Complete the three question self assessment to select a track.

CLICK

Do you believe in a heavenly divine savior?

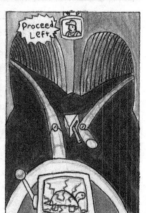

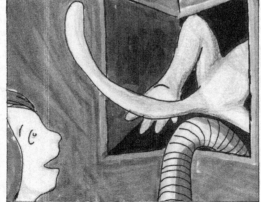

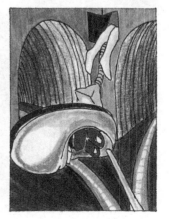

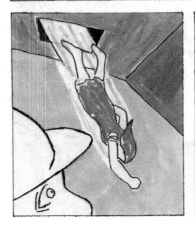

CHAPTER FOURTEEN

We begin with the ordeal.

To my left is a single feather taken from the Devil's advocate. I weigh creatures against this measure of evil to mete out justice.

On the right is a deli slicer.

All who are heavier than the feather contribute to our feast.

Which of you shall I weigh?

WAIT! I'll climb your ladder. She has important business with Samael.

Samael? Ugh. This is the second devil related case in a row.

Are we free to go now? We're in a hurry.

Child, there are procedures.

Defendant, state your name and the name of your co-defendant.

I'm Saklas! Doesn't anybody recognize me? And as for her, I don't know her name.

Since you give a false name, we will add you to the menu for lunch. We take names seriously,

and since your co-defendant has <u>no</u> name, that creature lacks all existence.

CHAPTER FIFTEEN

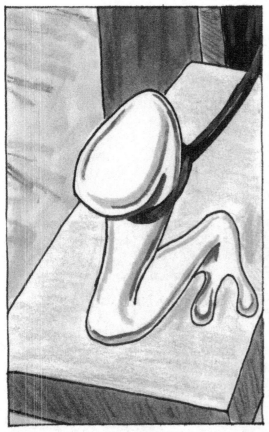

This is a safe place. There's nothing to fear. You can stop running.

But these fragmentary creatures—

This place can be overwhelming and frightening, but I wager you and I have compassion for the wounded in common.

Now let me explain this place while you catch your breath.

—Poor crow.—

74

During the great quake

our world

turned upside down.

This province was hit very hard.
I saw no survivors at first.

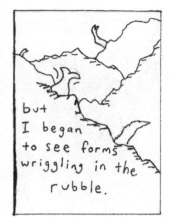

but I began to see forms wriggling in the rubble.

Somehow these odds and ends had survived, but they couldn't care for themselves,

So I cared for them.

I traded our sacred dogma of tyranny for gentle nurturing and protection.

For most this means safety and shelter,

but I lavish extra attention on as many as I can.

With enough affection they even begin to grow and become whole again.

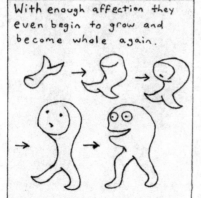

When they mature to that point, they no longer remain tethered.

It may seem like I am helping them, but in reality they are helping me.

75

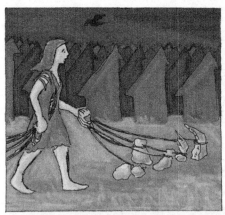

CHAPTER SIXTEEN

You aren't from around here are you?

How'd you guess?

Well, one doesn't see many abstainers in a hewnman eatery.

What do you imagine I'm abstaining from? And what is a hewnman?

I'll answer your questions, if if you tell me who you're hiding from.

It's a deal. You go first.

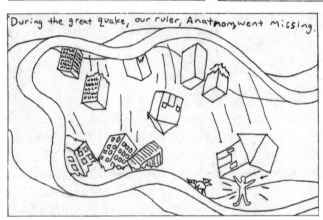

During the great quake, our ruler, Anatnom, went missing.

All the animals demanded a new ruler to restore order and rebuild the province.

Anatnom's closest companion was chosen to stand in his stead.

He behaved like Anatnom to the best of his ability.

Though it made him ill at first, he even went so far as to eat like him.

With each meal, he felt himself growing and changing.

80

He even felt himself becoming wiser.

I've known several creatures who spoke wise words, and none of them cannibalized their brothers.

This newly appointed ruler would disagree with your link between wisdom and words.

One is not proved wise by what comes out of his mouth,

Rather he is proved wise by what goes into it.

BLAH BLAH WORDS WORDS

And he never mentioned flesh or cannibalism. He coined a new term:

FOOD!

Sounds nice and neutral, right?

He ruled, rebuilt, and restored order at the cost of a few creatures.

He raised himself up a bit more with each one he cut down.

At some point he realized that eating never filled him. It only ever left him hungrier all the time.

Now I know what it means to be a man.

As he grew more similar to man with each kindred he ate, he felt something within him diminished, hewn away.

Thus he became the first hewn man.

How did there come to be so many hewn men?

FOOD $

Once the method of his transformation was revealed, all the animals clamoured for a cheap, guilt free, steady stream of food.

FOOD

That's when a creative entrepreneur stepped in to satisfy demand with ample provisions.

While this food was cheap, the new hewnmen soon learned that it comes with a steep hidden cost, hunger.

Before they - I mean **WE** - knew what had happened, they - I mean **WE** - were hooked.

We work hard for our daily food, but now we're all co-equal with men.

FOOD

Only our elected leader and the entrepreneur profit by our labor. We feel great pride from the freedom we have attained.

That's the story of hewnmen. Now tell me what you're running from.

The men accused me and my friend of being turtles and they tried to make us into their lunch.

Do you know somewhere I can hide for a while?

Sure. Come with me.

You're a much better listener than most hewnmen.

Stay as long as you like. I can provide you with all the creature comforts you desire.

If I am indeed a good listener, the moral of your story seems to be that satisfying all of one's desires is the problem, not the solution.

I just need a safe place to hide while I plot my next move.

82

Make yourself at home.

I've got to go to work. I'll be back soon.

...proud to be a self made, free hewnman.

Do you feel lost and alone? Depressed? Overweight? Try food. It worked for me.

Citizens, don't blame yourself for the hole in your soul that can't be filled. It is the men who brought us this pain.

It was Pall who originated the lust for food that beleaguers all of hewnman kind. He cursed us.

We all await the great day when hewnmen will rise up and slay the men for bringing tail, hunger, and the great quake upon us. Amen.

It has been really great to have a friendly face to come home to these last few days. Let's hang out when I get home from work today.

Uh huh.

When the divine feminine finally arrives in the world, She won't save us. She will judge and destroy us! Amen.

Who was it that said, "A caricature is putting the face of a joke on the body of a truth"?

?

Well boss, I don't know about all that, but if the farm keeps producing food at this rate, every last animal can be turned hewnman in no time.

It really is a shame.

I wish there was another way to hold a mirror up to my brothers' faces...

to show them their error! Alas, this caricature, these hewnmen, are the best I can do.

SPECIALTY MEATS

FREE CITY OF HEWNMEN—AN INDEPENDENT

CHAPTER SEVENTEEN

While we have toiled to rebuild according to the law of the book, they've been hiding out and playing games.

The old ways of the book stopped working for me. I wanted no part of all that nonsense anymore.

The twelve o'clock quake showed me the meaninglessness of our efforts. The futility of filling the infinite void within us struck me as a sick joke.

I feel sick.

Look Pal! Three blind mice,

Can't see how they run.

Always rushing higher,

but never having fun.

Three blind mice, ruling the book, by

BOOKS

they know that book is fishy, but prefer not to look.

One eats treats from crockery in excess and in blindness. The other dishes up mockery, and calls it hewnman kindness.

He is hooked on the same hunger that haunts men, and he's sick from not eating for a while.

Perhaps you feel that way but I haven't eaten a bite in a long time and I'm fine.

but I see what you mean.

It has been hours since fresh deliveries of food suddenly halted. This unforseeable famine is taking a toll on hewnmen all over.

Riots and protests have been widely reported as hungry hewnmen confront a feeling of deep discomfort and anxiety, cold sweats, and dread. One local business owner was quoted as saying, "I feel so sick right now, I'd eat anything that moves!" And that's exactly what a crowd of desperate rioters had in mind when they approached an unidentified creature outside of the Drool and Dine restaurant just moments ago. Somehow the creature has paralyzed the entire mob. The situation on the streets is extremely dangerous, citizens.

88

The supreme leader has made no media statement and cannot be reached for comment. He was last seen leaving the Independent Free State of Hewnmen with the CEO of Specialty Meat Foods late last night.

Boom! Boom!

We now return to coverage of the unidentified menace ravaging main street. The creature has entered a back corridor of the Drool and Dine restaurant.

SAKLAS, OPEN YOUR EYES.

Remember how you once lamented the knowledge that your toys were fashioned from the remains of your dead brothers?

And now look at you, hiding out in your charnel house with a throne and a poisoned scepter.

This is no place to sit and wait for the end.

Pall, we didn't come here to be the punchlines in your cat and mouse tales. We need the guidance of our eldest brother.

We are desperately divided.

You men fail to understand that I AM THE DIVIDING LINE...

between this world

MEN ARE MEAT

BULWARK IS BULLSH

and the Leviathan.

Do you even know how I raised the walls and secured the gate?

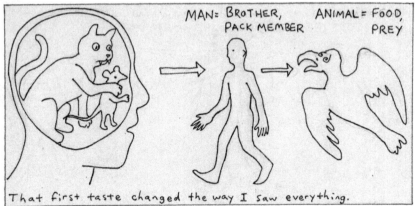

Then Saklas gave the great teaching of the crow.

Yum

A = animal, B = Saklas
If A is equal to B, then Saklas equals animal, food, prey.

Crow and I are cut from the same cloth. What you do to him — you do also to me.

This was the moment I lost control and the hunger overtook my better instincts.

-No!

Crow wait!

Right then a race began. I rushed to save the world before my hunger destroyed it.

The clock of history started ticking.

I locked Saklas out for his own protection and prepared the world to receive the divine savior.

We raised a whole civilization just to make ready.

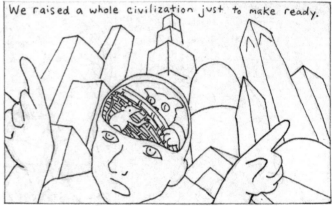

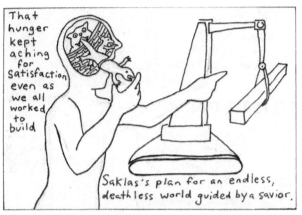

That hunger kept aching for satisfaction even as we all worked to build

Saklas's plan for an endless, deathless world guided by a savior.

Then came the day of the great quake. I was certain that the divine feminine would appear, so I prepared a fitting offering.

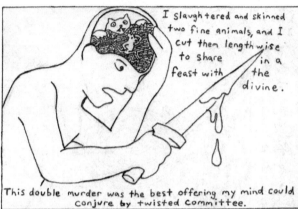

I slaughtered and skinned two fine animals, and I cut them lengthwise to share in a feast with the divine.

This double murder was the best offering my mind could conjure by twisted committee.

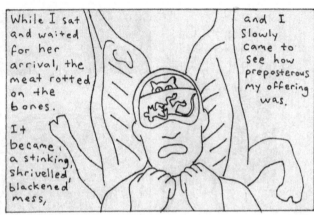

While I sat and waited for her arrival, the meat rotted on the bones.

It became a stinking, shrivelled, blackened mess,

and I slowly came to see how preposterous my offering was.

How could such a sacrifice ever appeal to a deity?

I moved past the hope that she would ever come save us during that long wait, and I moved past the hunger too. It just finally died.

Now some of you keep the laws of Saklas and some of you break them. As for me, I am above the law and I live on air alone.

I no longer wait for a savior or the end of history. My race is over. I am at rest.

CHAPTER EIGHTEEN

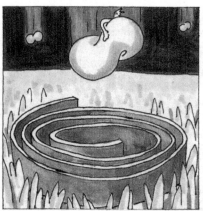

Pall.

Pall, look how you've grown.

Saklas, you are smaller, a more frail animal than I remembered, but I knew that voice before I even had eyes in my head. Welcome.

And you, highest of all divine forms, I am so sorry I doubted this moment would arrive. I lost hope that you would ever come for me.

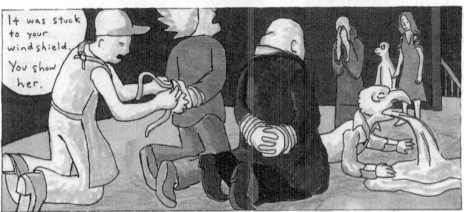

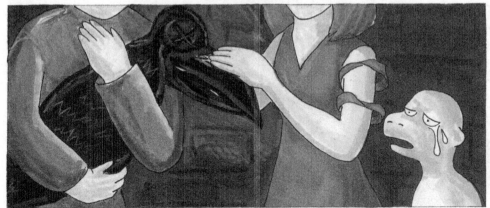

97

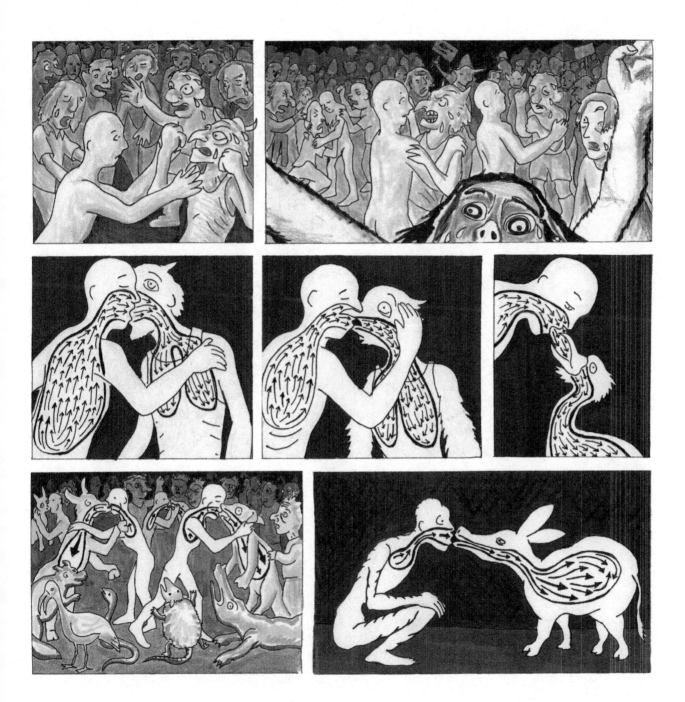

CHAPTER NINETEEN

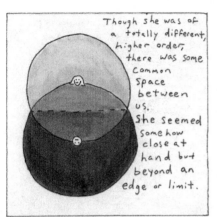

Though she was of a totally different, higher order, there was some common space between us. She seemed somehow close at hand but beyond an edge or limit.

Now I lay here in this lowest darkest place and she is unreachable. There can be no peace—no reconciliation from this distance.

This model bothers me greatly, because it appears so unlike our flat "leaf" ribbon world, but I have tested it against so many others and it rings the truest.

So it seems that light must remain entirely separate from darkness, the air will go out of every living thing, and all of you children will die.

Soon enough, only this sleeping monster and I will remain in the stale immortal blackness.

Your model is good, but incomplete. Look higher to put things in a fuller context. You'll reach a better conclusion

Everything you know was cut out and discarded from the higher world of light.

Here at the bottom, let's fold up this blackness above and below where you've fallen.

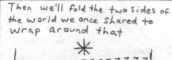

Then we'll fold the two sides of the world we once shared to wrap around that

Now here we are, separated from our higher origin and coiled as your giant curls up for a summer nap.

There is a way to reconcile and even to rise above this two sided, black and white world. We can leave this parade of ignorant beginnings, mortal ends, and eternal chaos.

My heavenly vision! I gave up on you. I was convinced that an endless sameness was my most optimistic of all possible outcomes.

What has finally brought you here?

If I can get the kashti, your little charm, there is a way for all of us to get beyond this torn fragment and repair what was broken.

Anything you say.

Watch! out

CHAPTER TWENTY

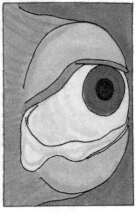

CHAPTER TWENTY-ONE

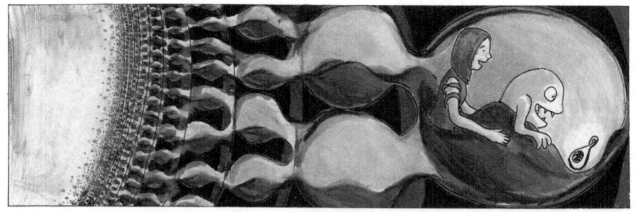

With good luck we've found your charm, but how do you intend to escape the bowels of the beast with it?

I never said I wanted to escape with it.

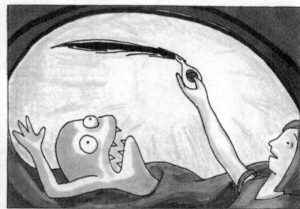

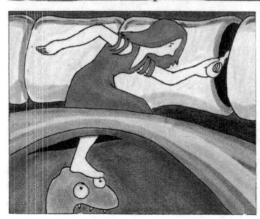

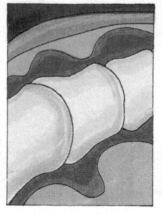

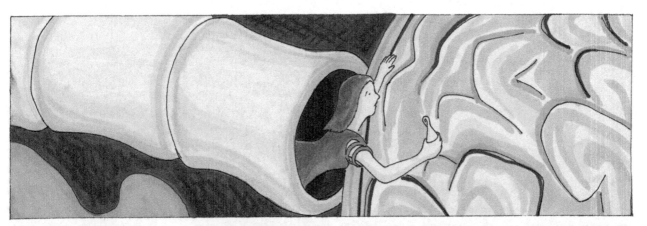

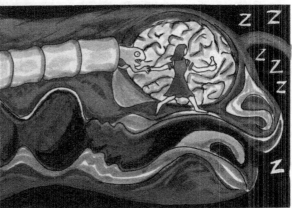

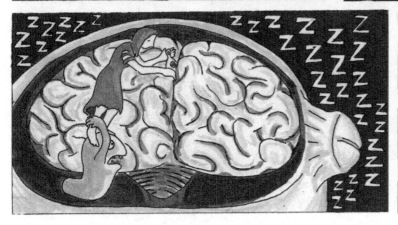

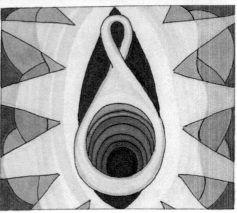

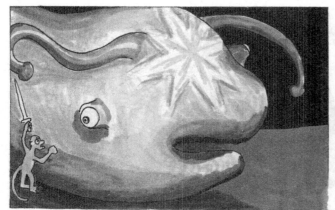

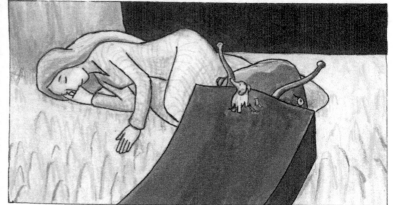

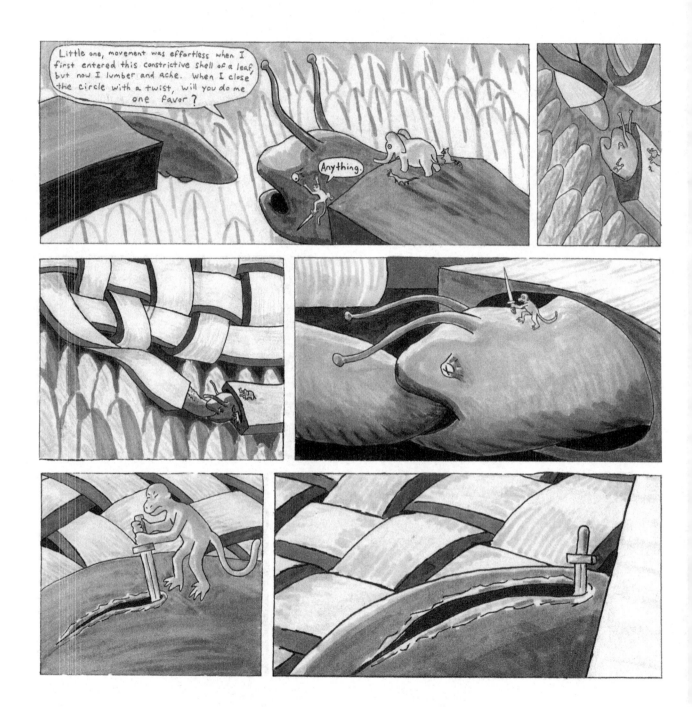

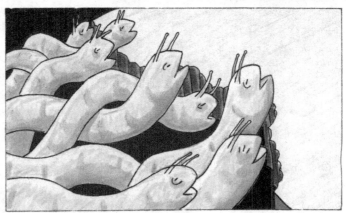

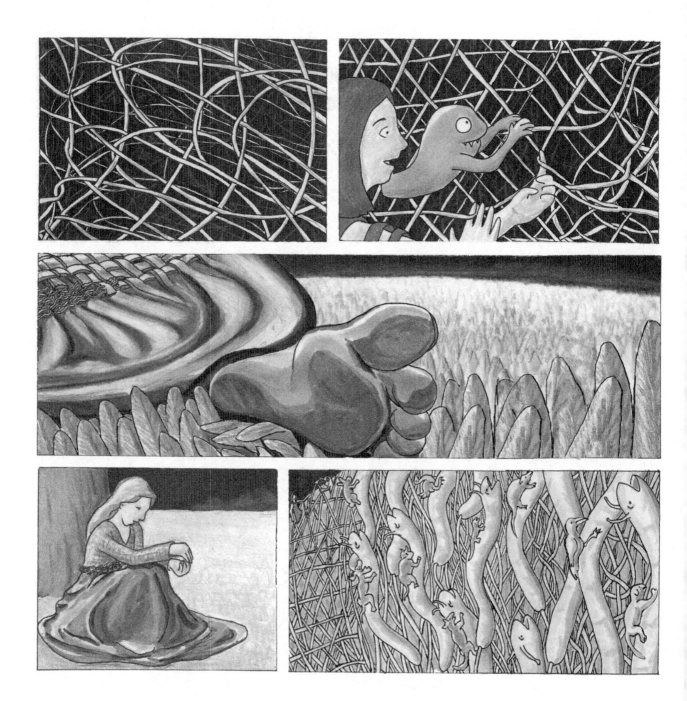

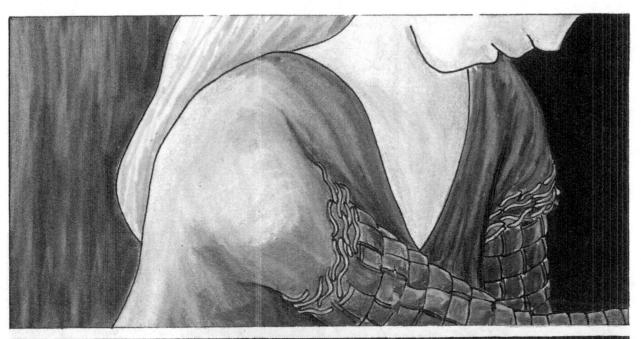

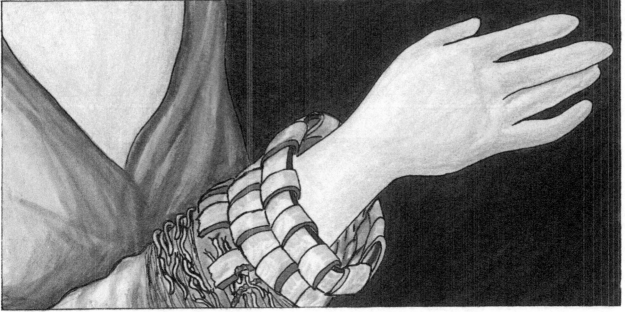

AFTERWORD

STEVAN L. DAVIES

Scott Finch's graphic novel, which he tells me reflects ideas found in my own book *The Secret Book of John: The Gnostic Gospel*, is the continuation of a three millennium long human effort to understand and explain the whole history of the universe as one continuous interconnected story with characters, plot, suspense and climactic events. One such story, which we call the Bible, became normative and canonical. To tell another cosmic story, or a mythic history that significantly deviated from that story,was eventually considered criminal activity, "heresy," sometimes punishable by death. Nevertheless, there have been dissenters from the canonical story. Some even declared that Moses had it wrong! In the Secret Book of John (aka the Apocryphon of John) the author extensively rewrites the canonical creation story, introducing some changes with the phrase "It was not as Moses said, but" his alternative version.

Such inventive people in the first centuries of the present era, from roughly 50 CE to 450 CE, are called Gnostics. A substantial library of Gnostic writing, their myths and stories and their novels of the history of the universe, was discovered in 1945 in Nag Hammadi, Egypt. Those books had been buried soon after 367 CE by the monks of a Christian monastery near Nag Hammadi because the bishop of Alexandria, Athanasius, had ordered that all monastic communities must burn all texts other than those of the canonical scriptures and the approved orthodox commentaries. Instead of burning theirs, some monks hid them, hoping to recover them when it was safe to do so. That day never came in their lifetimes.

The books of the Nag Hammadi library, and the other Gnostic books that survive, show that the ancient Gnostics demanded creativity. Scott Finch is part of this creative tradition and his views are similar in some ways to those of the ancient Gnostics of the first few centuries CE. His imaginative reconstruction of the history of the cosmos is a modern interpretation of theirs but featuring his own revelations.

Gnosticism has a dim view of the world, but not a dim view of reality. Gnostics believe that there is a divine reality beyond this apparent world and that we are the self-consciousness of God who has lost self-awareness. We are divine mind trapped in an illusory world that has no inherent reality and thus will disappear if we come to know it properly and begin, as Jesus says in the Gospel of Thomas (11, 111), to live from the living and arrive in the light. In order to break the "fall" of God into being us and to return to primordial divine self-knowledge, a Gnostic had to comprehend the process of his own fall into objectivity and alienation. The history of the cosmos is the history of God's mind, and this is the history of every individual. Psychogeny recapitulates cosmogeny. It would be incumbent upon and therapeutic for any Gnostic to re-write the story of God in his own narrative language, to trace his own fall and return by a cosmological myth. In this sense Gnostic myth is autobiography. To know your own cosmic story is a factor in salvation according to the Gnostics, and to tell your story is to generate myth that may facilitate the salvation of others.

CREATIVITY

The ancient Gnostics demanded creativity. Scott Finch's imaginative reconstruction of the history of the cosmos is the modern interpretation of theirs, not the same as theirs, but part of the same quest. For Gnosticism there was a general pattern for myths of origin, one that is classically exemplified in the Secret Book of John, but unorthodox ancient writers felt free to revise and extend, complicate or simplify, the cosmology of the world as they saw fit. Their creativity shocked orthodox Christian writers. One of the earliest orthodox opponents of the Gnostic writings, Bishop Irenaeus of Lyon in Gaul wrote about Gnostics in ca. 180 C.E. that "every one of them generates something new, day by day, according to his ability; for no one is deemed 'perfect,' who does not develop among them some mighty fictions" (Irenaeus: *Against Heresies*, 1:18). Irenaeus has no respect for individual creativity, it is a threat to church order. He is the earliest known source for an idea that eventually came to be beyond discussion, that there are and can be four and only four Gospels and that further creativity in that regard is absolutely unacceptable. (*AH*, 3:11).

Irenaeus also writes against any proliferation of individual mythic constructions: "Many offshoots of numerous heresies have already been formed from those heretics we have described. . . . They insist upon teaching something new, declaring themselves the inventors of any sort of opinion which they may have been able to call into existence" (*AH*, 1:28). It makes sense in a social-Darwinist way that a strongly heirarchical orthodox church organization would more easily survive through the centuries than a movement insisting on the creative freedom of individuals. It makes social sense, but we don't have to like it.

Today, as the institutional church very slowly breaks down and loses its ability to enforce uniformity, creativity is coming back to life in the worlds of religious mythic construction. Scott Finch is creating new myth as the Gnostic mythicists did two thousand years ago. His work is part of a great lineage.

CARNIVORES

In this Gnostic novel Scott Finch shares his vision with all of us. His vision is somewhat more inclusive than the old Gnostic myths were because he is particularly concerned with the role and fate of animals and birds while they, in typical human fashion, ancient writers were interested almost entirely in human beings. Scott Finch is interested in creating a myth of life, not just of human life.

The question of human relations with animals does occasionally arise in ancient Gnostic thinking. In the Gospel of Thomas there are sayings attributed to Jesus that are concerned with issues raised by the consumption of animal flesh by humans. Since this matter is one Scott Finch considers seriously in this graphic novel, I will address it briefly here.

We read in the Gospel of Thomas saying 60:"They saw a Samaritan going into Judea carrying a lamb. Jesus asked his disciples: 'What do you think he will do with that lamb?' They replied, 'He'll kill it and eat it.' He said to them, 'As long as it remains alive he will not eat it; only if he kills it and it becomes a corpse. They said: 'Otherwise he won't be able to do so.' He said to them: 'You too must seek a place for rest or you may become a corpse and be eaten.'" This curious anecdote tells us that people eat the meat of dead animals, not living ones, but everyone already knows that. When we are told something utterly obvious, we can sometimes infer that there is something more subtle being said than the surface indicates. And indeed we also hear Jesus say in saying 11, "This sky will cease to be and the sky above it will cease to be. The dead do not live, and the living will not die. When you ate dead things you made them alive. When you arrive into light what will you do?" Here the theme goes a little further; people surely do eat dead animals and then the dead animals are transformed into living people. But this is not enough, because how can we ensure that we while living will not die? If we arrive in the light and attain enlightenment then, implicitly, eating dead things will no longer be appropriate for us.

Thomas' gospel is often about transformation. In saying 22 we hear in part that "When you make an eye to replace an eye, and a hand to replace a hand, and a foot to replace a foot, and an image to replace an image then you will enter the Kingdom." So if this sky (or this "heaven") and the sky above it cease to be, and presumably are replaced by even higher skies, and if we as human beings are transformed into a new body and a new image (of God), we will evidently no longer need to be carnivores. People have long eaten dead things and transformed them into themselves who are living. What happens, Jesus asks, when you yourself arrive into light and are beyond merely living? "When you ate dead things you made them alive. When you arrive into light what will you do?"

We have something of an answer to this question in saying 111 where we hear that Jesus said: "The earth and sky will roll up right in front of you. Anyone living from the living will not die. Doesn't Jesus say that the world is not worthy of one who finds himself?" People who are transformed, whose worldly sky has rolled up and been replaced by a higher sky and greater earth, such a person will not live from the corpses of dead animals but will live from the living divinity and never die. He or she has achieved the ultimate gnostic goal: divine self-knowledge.

Now people are kept alive by eating the flesh of dead animals, when they come into the light they should live in another way. Jesus criticizes carnivorous human behavior especially clearly in saying 87, "Wretched is a body depending on a body and wretched is a soul depending on these two." How does a body depend on a body? By killing it and eating it for, as Jesus said of the Samaritan's lamb in saying 60, "as long as it remains alive he will not eat it; only if he kills it and it becomes a corpse," and anyone who eats a corpse inhabits a body dependent on a body and so is spiritually wretched.

The question is then, as Jesus put it, "when you ate dead things you made them alive. When you arrive into light what will you do?" You should no longer live on dead things but on the living, for "anyone living from the living will not die." And exactly how will we do that? I can't say. But Jesus does say, in the canonical tradition, (Luke 12:29-31) "Do not set your heart on what you will eat or drink; do not worry about it. For the pagan world runs after all such things, and your Father knows that you need them. But seek his kingdom, and these things will be given to you as well." Whether this advice is serviceable is unclear. What is clear is that the tradition conveyed by the Gospel of Thomas is concerned with the contradiction between humans who seek light and God's kingdom and the lifestyle of humans who kill animals and consume them for food. I believe that Scott Finch shows similar concern in his graphic novel. The only way to appreciate his novel is to read it. It stands in a long tradition of alternative visions of cosmic human history and thus it does not stand alone. Enjoy.

Stevan L. Davies is Professor of Religious Studies at Misericordia University. His work includes *The Gospel of Thomas and Christian Wisdom* (Second Edition, Bardic Press) and *The Secret Book of John: The Gnostic Gospel Annotated and Explained* (Skylight Paths Publishing).

NOTE

As this book took shape, I happened upon John Donne's "Holy Sonnet V: I am a Little World Made Cunningly." The way this poem mirrored, outlined, and expanded on everything I had set out to express was startling. It became an armature and touchstone for my convoluted tale. I hope devotees of Donne will forgive one necessary twist by a character in my story as he exchanges the words "O Lord" for "Lady." This little switch reverses a trick that's been played ever since the divine took shape in our mind's eye as an old man in the clouds.

CPSIA information can be obtained
at www.ICGtesting.com
Printed in the USA
LVOW03s1804290816
502330LV00016B/590/P